Un

by Elspeth O'Neill

THE MEDICI SOCIETY LTD
LONDON
1986

One day, on the way home from school, Daisy, Blossom and Sam went to see their Uncle Sylvester. He was an artist, and lived in an old house at Buttercup Green.

Usually, Uncle Sylvester was painting in his studio, but this time he was sitting at the kitchen table, looking sad. A supply of their favourite home-made biscuits was kept in a tin for his nephew and nieces, but Uncle Sylvester had bad news. 'The biscuit tin is empty,' he said. 'I have no money left to buy biscuits or, indeed, paints and canvases.' Daisy, Blossom and Sam could not believe their Uncle, but when he opened the tin it was empty.

Uncle Sylvester explained that all his money had gone on repairing the roof of the old house which had begun to leak during last week's storm. Daisy, Blossom and Sam were very upset. 'Can we help you, Uncle? There must be something we can do', said Sam. Uncle Sylvester shook his head saying, 'I could probably sell a painting or two in the city, but I can't afford the train fare to take them to the exhibition'. Uncle Sylvester looked unhappy and the young geese sadly left him.

When Daisy, Blossom and Sam reached their home in Farmer Bloomfield's orchard Matilda, their mother, had ready their favourite tea of bread and honey and cakes. They began to feel more cheerful!

They told their mother all about Uncle Sylvester's troubles and how, on their way home, they had made plans to help him. They knew exactly how to get Uncle Sylvester's paintings shown at the exhibition.

Tom, Farmer Bloomfield's nephew, was a guard on the train which went every day to the city from Buttercup Green station. He had often promised the young geese a ride in the guard's van and now here was their chance. Their mother couldn't think why anybody should want to go to the city, as the bustle and noise there made her feathers quiver and her beak chatter alarmingly. But she was very fond of her brother Sylvester and wanted to help him. So she and Daisy, Blossom and Sam spent the rest of the evening taking their favourite paintings off the walls and packing them very carefully. The young geese then went to bed earlier than usual so as to be awake in good time.

Next day, Daisy, Blossom and Sam hurried down the hill to catch the 9 o'clock train.

Tom quickly found them a comfortable seat on some empty sacks in a corner of the guard's van. They were very excited and, when the train drew into the station in the big city, just a little bit scared.

Tom showed Daisy, Blossom and Sam where to get the underground train to take them to the exhibition hall. The other passengers were curious at the unusual sight of three chattering geese carrying such awkward parcels.

Daisy, Blossom and Sam scrambled off the underground train at the correct station and waddled on to the escalator which carried them and the large, precious parcels up to the street.

The exhibition hall was opposite the station and, carefully crossing the busy street, Sam rushed up the steps, quickly followed by Blossom and Daisy.

A distinguished-looking old gentleman came forward to meet the geese. Daisy began to unwrap her favourite picture of Strawberry Hill and the old man beamed with pleasure when he saw it. He was even more delighted when Sam showed him the painting he had chosen of Mrs Bloomfield, sitting in her armchair reading by lamplight.

Poor Blossom was so flustered she held up her picture back-to-front and, instead of the pretty view of the orchard, all the old gentleman could see were splodges of paint where Uncle Sylvester had been mixing colours. The others quickly helped her turn it round, and when the old gentleman saw the view of the orchard, he immediately began to clap his hands. He jumped up and down with excitement and chuckled to himself.

The old gentleman asked Sam to write Uncle
Sylvester's name and address on a large piece
of paper, and also to sign his own name.
Daisy and Blossom watched as he wrote
'Samuel Gander' in his best joined-up hand-
writing.

Then, with a polite goodbye to the old
gentleman, who looked extremely happy,
Daisy, Blossom and Sam skipped down the
steps to the street. A very kind policeman
showed them where to catch a bus to take
them to the station. He explained that if they
travelled on top of an open double-decker
bus they would see more of the city.

Sitting on the top deck, the other passengers pointed out all the interesting sights to Sam, Daisy and Blossom as the bus rumbled to the station.

Tom was waiting for them by the train, and in what seemed no time at all they were stepping out of the guard's van on to the platform at Buttercup Green station.

Matilda, their mother, was so glad to see them back safe and sound that she hugged each of them in turn.

The days passed slowly. Matilda packed a basket of food each day for Uncle Sylvester. In it was a loaf of home-baked bread, some cheese and fruit, and she also made a large bowl of hot soup for the geese to take to their Uncle. Sometimes he painted in his studio, but more often he could be found painting by the river in Farmer Bloomfield's orchard.

But poor Uncle Sylvester grew more worried as each day it was harder and harder to squeeze even a tiny drop of paint from the silver tubes, and he had used up almost all his canvases.

Then, one sunny morning, the postman brought Uncle Sylvester a large white envelope.

Nervously, Uncle Sylvester drew out a card bordered in gold. He read his name, Sylvester Gander. Next −in gold letters− 'Two thousand pounds awarded to Sylvester Gander−First Prize for painting *The Orchard* in the Summer Exhibition'.

He couldn't believe his eyes. How had his painting got to the exhibition? He thought Matilda had that particular painting in her cottage. He was puzzled. He hurried off to see her and to tell her the exciting news.

On the way, he dashed into the art shop with a long list of much-needed paints and canvases, arranging to collect them later. He hurried past all the cows and sheep and soon reached the orchard. Matilda was delighted to learn of the prize and Daisy, Blossom and Sam danced about with excitement. Sam asked if he could see the letter with the news. When he read it he noticed another piece of paper pinned to the back of the letter. He went quite dizzy with shock for it said that Sylvester had also won the second prize of One Thousand pounds for the painting of *A lady reading by lamplight*. The Committee wanted very much to meet the brilliant, but unknown, artist. Very soon!

Uncle Sylvester had to hear first how his nephew and nieces had taken the paintings which he had given to Matilda up to the exhibition .

Then Matilda told Uncle Sylvester that she would make him a new blue smock to wear on this grand occasion and Daisy, Blossom and Sam would ask Tom to let him sit in the guard's van on the train. Matilda could see that Uncle Sylvester was feeling very, very nervous!

But next day, Uncle Sylvester, wearing his new smock, looked very much happier as he went off to the city, and the geese waved and waved until the train was out of sight.

Soon Uncle Sylvester was climbing up the steps of the exhibition hall. Imagine the surprise on the faces of all the important people, including the old gentleman, when they discovered that Sylvester Gander, who had won the two most important prizes of the year, was a most handsome clever GOOSE !

The newspapers next day were full of the story, with photographs of him with the prize-winning paintings. He also appeared on the television news!

From then on Uncle Sylvester had no problems selling his paintings. He became world-famous and his pictures were to be found in many galleries where people smiled to see such happy and colourful paintings. Uncle Sylvester could now afford to buy all the paints and canvases he wanted, and he knew he owed it all to Daisy, Blossom and Sam.

You can be sure, too, that the biscuit tin was never empty again!